Never Wash your Hair

MARGARET McALLISTER

Illustrated by Tim Archbold

OXFORD
UNIVERSITY PRESS

OXFORD
UNIVERSITY PRESS

Great Clarendon Street, Oxford OX2 6DP

Oxford University Press is a department of the University of Oxford.
It furthers the University's objective of excellence in research, scholarship,
and education by publishing worldwide in

Oxford   New York

Auckland   Cape Town   Dar es Salaam   Hong Kong   Karachi
Kuala Lumpur   Madrid   Melbourne   Mexico City   Nairobi
New Delhi   Shanghai   Taipei   Toronto

With offices in

Argentina   Austria   Brazil   Chile   Czech Republic   France   Greece
Guatemala   Hungary   Italy   Japan   Poland   Portugal   Singapore
South Korea   Switzerland   Thailand   Turkey   Ukraine   Vietnam

Oxford is a registered trade mark of Oxford University Press
in the UK and in certain other countries

British Library Cataloguing in Publication Data
Data available

ISBN: 978-0-19-918419-4

7 9 10 8

Available in packs
Stage 14 More Stories A Pack of 6:
ISBN: 978-0-19-918416-3
Stage 14 More Stories A Class Pack:
ISBN: 978-0-19-918423-1
Guided Reading Cards also available:
ISBN: 978-0-19-918425-5

Cover artwork by Tim Archbold

Printed in China by Imago

Paper used in the production of this book is a natural,
recyclable product made from wood grown in sustainable forests.
The manufacturing process conforms to the environmental
regulations of the country of origin.

CHAPTER 1

The thing in the water

Headlice live in clean hair. Everyone tells you that. If you don't want headlice, don't wash your hair.

Parents don't understand that. They make you wash your hair, then they complain because you get nits. And I didn't even have any!

I had something else, though.

'There's no shame in having nits,' said Mum, 'so long as you do something about them.'

She was certainly doing something about them. She had me under arrest in the bathroom, with a towel round my neck.

There was steam rising from the hot water in the wash-basin, and the mirror was misting over. She pulled on a pair of white plastic gloves, like a doctor.

'I'm twelve,' I said. 'I don't need you to wash my hair.'

'You do today,' she said.

Next thing I knew my head was in the water and so was most of the towel, and she was rubbing this vile-smelling shampoo – it's called Nit-Death or something – into my head.

When I sat up, I found a dry bit of towel to rub my face with, then I dried the mirror to see what she was doing.

She was bent over my head, searching through my hair.

She had a fixed expression on her face, like a cat at a bird box.

It wasn't so much the look that scared me, it was the nit comb in her hand. I've got curly brown hair, and it hurts when it gets combed. Especially when Mum does it.

'Ow!' I yelled. It wasn't hurting yet, but I wanted to remind her that I was in there.

'I'm sure these are nits,' said Mum. She raked away with the comb.

'Ouch!' Then I stopped and said nothing. I just sat with my mouth open, looking at the water in the wash-basin.

Something was swimming in there. It wasn't a headlouse. It wasn't much bigger than an ant, but it was definitely swimming, the way a human swims, with arms and legs.

It had a tawny brown body, and its arms seemed too long for it. It had a long tail, too.

'At least I think these are nits,' said Mum. She didn't sound so sure. 'Is there a magnifying glass in your bedroom?'

'There's my bug viewer,' I said. 'There's a magnifying lens in there.' My eyes were still on the creature. It was nearly at the side of the basin, and it was slowing down.

Mum went away to find the bug viewer.

The creature put out one arm, then the other, and tried to climb up the side of the wash-basin, but there was nothing for it to grip. It scrabbled about and fell back, so I saw its face, and a white patch on its front. It was too exhausted to go on swimming.

I put my finger in the water, just as Mum came in with the lens. She peered into my hair.

'Funny,' she muttered. 'These are the wrong shape for nits. Wrong colour, too. Curvy and greeny-yellow. Like bananas, only smaller.'

'Can I have the lens, please, Mum?' I said.

The creature had crawled on to my finger, and was shaking itself dry. Then it stopped, and I could feel my heart beating harder and faster. It was rubbing its face with its paws, or hands. I could see its long arms, its sad, ugly, funny face, and its tail.

'There's something moving in there!' said Mum.

She dived at my head, scooped up something with the comb, and dropped it into the bug viewer. 'Give me the lens, Tom, quickly!'

She jammed on the lid, but I was still looking at the creature on my finger. It was crouched down, turning its head one way and then the other. Mum noticed it, too.

'That's another one,' she said. 'It must be some kind of headlouse. Where on earth have you been, to pick these up?'

'Just school,' I said. 'And Nick and I went looking for red squirrels last weekend. Are you going to ring his mum?'

'I'll have to,' she said, 'in case Nick's caught them, too. Don't worry, I'm sure she won't tell anyone. But if you've got nits, she needs to know.'

'No, Mum,' I said.

'Sorry, but she has to be told.'

'I meant, no, I haven't got nits. I've got head monkeys. Look!'

CHAPTER 2

When the doctor went bananas

I suppose Mum was upset. Parents don't like their kids to have passengers – especially Mum.

I'd love a pet – a dog would be best – but Mum doesn't like having animals around the place.

Nick's family got a dog from the rescue centre. I'd like one, but I know what Mum would say.

Anyway, watching the monkeys was as good as having a pet. By the time we'd finished combing out my hair, we had five in the bug viewer.

One was a bit bigger than the others, and paler, and I called it Kong. The tiniest one was Tich, and the three in between were Rag, Tag and Bobtail.

They were scampering about in there, trying to climb up the sides, and wondering where my hair had gone.

Mum was sitting on the side of the bath, holding on as if she was afraid she'd faint and fall in.

'Doctor!' she said at last. 'We'll see the doctor. Then Nick's mother. Tom, get your coat.'

We had a long wait to see the doctor, and I was worried. I didn't dare let the monkeys out of the bug viewer, but they didn't like it.

They had nothing to eat in there, and nothing to play with. I kept them covered up in my jacket in the waiting room so nobody would see them.

The doctor looked bored out of his mind when we first went in. I suppose he'd been looking down people's ears all afternoon.

So we told him what I was there for, and it really made his day.

I showed him the monkeys and he sort of jibbered to himself. Then he looked up and jibbered at me, then he jibbered at the monkeys and they jibbered back.

They didn't look happy. They were jumping up and down and squeaking, and trying to find a way out of the bug viewer.

They'd been all right in my hair. Animals are like that.

Nick and I go out watching wildlife a lot.

We know where to see birds, deer, hedgehogs, shrews, anything.

We'd just been out on Saturday to look for red squirrels at – well, never mind where. You have to be patient with wild animals. They're shy. If anything upsets them, they head for cover and hide. They wanted my hair to hide in.

'Amazing,' said the doctor. 'It must be a new species.' Then before you could say *bananas* he was on the phone to some professor somewhere, and chattering away as if he was talking monkey-speak himself.

When he'd finished, he swivelled round in his chair and said, 'Professor McAndrew from the university will come to your school to see you in the morning. In the meantime, you must say nothing about this. This is all top secret until you've seen Professor McAndrew.'

'There won't be anything for Professor McThing to see,' I said. 'Not if they stay in the bug viewer all night. Look at them!'

The monkeys had stopped jumping about. Rag, Tag and Bobtail had hidden their faces in their arms and were sulking. Kong had picked up Tich and was rocking him from side to side. The doctor took a close look at them.

'They were healthy, were they, when they left your head?'

'Oh, yes. Wet through, though.'

'Then they'd better go back there,' he said.

Mum complained that she'd just got them out, but he tipped them over my head and watched to see how they settled in.

It was really frustrating. The doctor was standing there saying, 'Look, they're eating bananas! He's making a nest!' and I couldn't see a thing. All I knew about was a tickly feeling above my right ear.

At home, Mum rounded up my two
sisters and checked their hair, but she
didn't find anything. Hardly surprising.

They both use so much spray and
mousse and stuff, they've got hair like
paper maché.

And Dad's got a head like a skating
rink.

Mum had just finished when the
phone rang, and I went to answer it. It
was Nick's mother, and she was having
hysterics.

CHAPTER 3

His name's Pedro

The doctor must have phoned school. As soon as I got there in the morning, the secretary sent me to the medical room to wait for Professor McAndrew.

Nick was in there already, grinning all over his face. I could see why the monkeys had chosen Nick. His hair's even curlier than mine and it's ginger. It looks like a rusty Brillo pad.

It was good to know that Nick was in this with me.

The doctor had told me not to tell anyone about the micro-monkeys, but he needn't have worried. It's not the sort of thing you shout about in the school yard, is it? But it's different with your best mate.

Nick and I had spent so many weekends crawling about, observing wild animals, and now we had our own crop of monkeys. Nobody else could have understood how we felt.

'Bet you didn't brush your hair this morning,' said Nick.

He looked into my hair, and the next minute he was chuckling away to himself and muttering 'Wow' and 'Look at that!'

'I can't,' I said. 'Shove off, Nick, it's my turn.'

I got him to sit down so I could see the monkeys in his hair.

It's as near to a jungle as you'll find on this side of Africa.

It was amazing. Wonderful. Brilliant. Think of the best word you know. Double it. It was like that.

There were two of them, paler than my monkeys, and so tiny they could have hidden behind a grain of rice. You could see their gentle monkey faces, and their gangly arms and legs.

They were swinging from one hair to another, graceful and strong, and never falling. They'd made a slide down the back of his head, and they took turns whizzing down on their backs and climbing up again.

They never lost their balance. Just when you thought they'd fall over, they'd flick their tails round a hair and pull themselves up.

And you know those nits that looked like bananas? They really were bananas. I suppose anything could grow in Nick's hair, or mine.

I saw a little monkey pull one off the bunch. He peeled it, munched it, and searched inside the skin to see if there was anything else in there. Then he sat on it and slid down the back of Nick's neck.

It must have been a fast banana skin.

It gathered speed, whizzing towards Nick's collar, and I thought the monkey would vanish down there. But as the banana skin sped out of control, the monkey leapt sideways and landed on my wrist.

He crouched there, looking from side to side. At last, he looked up. His eyes were deep and dark, and he was so tiny. I wished I had a magnifying lens with me. He had a hopeful, trusting look, like a faithful dog. I wanted to take care of him.

I don't suppose he could see me properly, but he looked straight at me. He was alone and not sure where he was, but he wasn't afraid.

'What's going on?' asked Nick. I showed him the monkey on my hand.

'He fell off,' I said. 'His name's Pedro.' It just was. 'And the other one's Peppy.'

The door opened, and the woman who walked in was small, quite young, black, and pretty. She was wearing jeans, and a sweatshirt with a picture of a dolphin. She had a bag like a rucksack over one shoulder.

I hid Pedro under my hand.

'Tom Pringle and Nick Jackson?' she said. 'I'm Angela McAndrew, from the university.'

I don't know what we'd expected Professor McAndrew to be like. Maybe a big hairy Scotsman or a dotty old butterfly hunter. We hadn't imagined anyone like this.

She put her bag over the back of a chair, and said, 'I'd like to see the monkeys, please.'

She said it as if it was perfectly normal, and she was polite. She didn't just take it for granted that she could root about in our hair.

I put Pedro back on to Nick's head.

She leaned forward to watch. I saw the fascination on her face, like a little kid looking at a Christmas tree. When I saw her look at them like that, I knew they'd be safe with her.

It was a good thing I knew it. Things didn't seem too safe after that.

CHAPTER 4

The eye of a monster

She said they were miniature macaque monkeys. Goodness knows how she could tell. To people like her, a new type of monkey is like landing on Mars and winning the World Cup, all in one.

There was a lot of telephoning our parents, then we were each sent home to pack a weekend bag.

It seemed that Nick and I were an SSSI. That means Site of Special Scientific Interest. If you say it means 'sissy', I'll flatten you. You're not allowed to disturb an SSSI. You're not allowed to dig it up, plough it, or trespass on it either.

An SSSI is also allowed off school. Nick and I had to go to the university with Professor McAndrew, but by the time we got there, she'd told us to call her 'Angela'.

The university is dull to look at, greyish-white like council offices.

We were walking across the car park when Angela said, 'Will you two miss anything important, if you have to stay over the weekend?'

'We were going to look for squirrels,' I said.

'Squirrels?' She sounded really interested.

'Red ones,' I said. 'We've found a place where you can sometimes see them. We go to …'

Nick jabbed me in the ribs.

'Er – we go to see if there's any around,' I finished. We were at the main door by then.

A security guard waved us through when he saw Angela. She took us in and out of a lift, and along miles of corridors until we stopped outside a door.

'You're going to meet Professor Barron and Sir George Montgomery,' she said.

'They're expecting you. They've been told about the monkeys.' She gave an encouraging smile. 'Don't worry.'

Then she opened the door, and we were in the grey box. It wasn't really a grey box, but that's how it looked.

The walls were grey and white, and the carpet was cold porridge colour.

In the middle of the room, two men sat on dark grey swivel chairs.

The one who stood up to meet us was very thin, with a grey beard and glasses. His clothes looked too big for him.

'This is Professor Barron,' said Angela.

'He's in charge of the labs. He's Head of Research.'

Barron the Boffin, I thought. He smiled, but I felt he wanted to slice me up and put me under a microscope.

'And this,' said Angela, 'is Sir George Montgomery.'

I recognized him, because I'd seen him on television. He was big and bald and very rich. He smiled as if his eyes didn't know what his mouth was doing.

'Are you Sir George from Montgomery Network?' asked Nick. Of course he was.

Montgomery Network is his company. He owns cinemas and a film company, and he's something to do with cable TV. Monty the Money. I wondered what he had to do with the university.

'Sir George has been very generous,' said Angela, as if she knew what I was thinking.

'We couldn't go on without Sir George,' said Barron the Boffin. 'The department depends on his help.'

What he meant was – don't upset the Moneybags. It looked as if Sir George Money Montgomery thought he could buy and sell us all. What price would a few monkeys fetch?

He was already squinting at the top of my head without as much as 'please may I?' He reached out his big hairy hand, with gold rings on his fat fingers.

'The monkeys are very delicate,' said Angela, quickly. 'And they may bite.'

Moneybags took a step back. Barron the Boffin took out a pair of white plastic gloves, and eased them on.

'Excuse me,' said Angela. She put her hand lightly on top of my head, and lifted it away again with Kong and Tich on her finger.

Boffin took a lens from his pocket and stared at the monkeys. That was scary.

Through the glass his eye looked like the eye of a monster, and the monkeys looked tinier than ever.

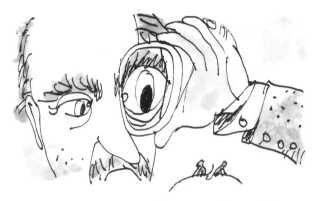

He was only the first. It should have been exciting, but I've never been so bored. All these scientists came in and peered at the monkeys.

Boffin asked us where we'd been. I was just about to say we'd been squirrel-watching when I saw Angela, shaking her head.

'We were just mucking about,' I said. 'At the park.'

He didn't ask any more. He just looked over his glasses at Angela and said, 'Do we have a place in the lab tonight, for the specimens?'

Specimens? I didn't know if he meant the monkeys or us.

'Certainly not,' said Angela. 'The monkeys show signs of distress when they're taken from the boys' heads.'

'So we need to put these boys in a lab,' said Boffin.

'The boys are staying with me,' said Angela. 'I'm taking them home now. You can do your observations tomorrow.'

'We need to do more than observations,' said Barron the Boffin, and he gave Angela a chilly stare. 'We shall set up ...'

'We're going home,' said Angela. 'Come on, Tom, Nick. We'll get a pizza on the way back.'

Angela's flat was far better than the university.

We phoned home, ate loads of pizza, played computer games, and watched Phil Jenkinson videos. He's brilliant.

He's big and hairy and loud, and he does wildlife programmes. Picture a cross between Father Christmas and a bird's nest. That's Phil Jenkinson.

Angela was at university with him! She said he lives near here and they still work together sometimes, lucky thing.

She had the bright idea of moving the monkeys on to her own head for a while. Then Nick and I could both watch them.

Rag, Tag and Bobtail escaped back to me when I was bending down to look. They came out again with bunches of bananas. I think they wanted to set up a plantation on Angela.

She made up beds on the floor for me and Nick, and we lay awake for ages, watching the monkeys by torchlight.

I didn't tell Nick the thing I was worrying about. I was trying to forget it. It was the look in the Boffin's monster eye when he saw the monkeys.

We went back to the university in the morning. Angela took us to the door of the grey box, but when she heard all the noise, she stopped us. There was a huge row going on.

I could hear Barron the Boffin sounding short and snappy. Moneybags was blustering and bullying.

'Science means money!' Moneybags was shouting. 'I've been on the Internet half the night, and I've had three offers already. We can sell the cartoon rights and the advertising rights, and Micro-Monkey toys. And the film rights!

'Do you want money, or don't you? This place doesn't pay for itself! What about a Micro-Monkeys Exhibition?'

'We can't plan anything,' said Boffin sharply. 'We need to observe these creatures in the lab. We don't know yet if they can survive away from the boys' heads. We need to try them on different diets. We don't know what other kinds of food they'll eat. There are seven of them, so we can afford to lose the odd one. We need at least one dead one, for dissection.'

I thought of Pedro, and tried not to. I felt sick. Angela's eyes betrayed her rage. It was terrifying.

'... And we need to know where the boys picked these things up,' went on Boffin. 'There must be a whole colony of these monkeys somewhere.'

'Wildlife films,' said Moneybags. 'And a shampoo! That boy said his mother washed his hair with Dichlorodeth shampoo, and the monkeys survived! Those monkeys may be rare now, but we could end up with thousands! We'll need a pesticide to get rid of them. We must make one before anybody else does. Get one or two of those monkeys in the lab, and find something that kills them.'

'The first thing is to get the monkeys away from those boys,' said Boffin. His voice was coming nearer to the door.

'Where's Angela? She should be here by now.'

Angela pushed open the nearest door and shoved us through it.

It turned out to be the men's loo. Luckily there was nobody else in there.

We'd just closed the door behind us when we heard Moneybags thumping along the corridor, shouting for us.

'If he thinks,' said Angela, 'that he can turn the monkeys into a circus act, he's mistaken. And Professor Barron isn't going to experiment on them. It's time I got you out of here.'

She heaved open the window, and looked down.

'Fire escape. Fast.'

One at a time we slid through the window and scarpered down the fire escape.

Then we ran for Angela's car.

'Are we going back to your flat?' asked Nick, as we strapped ourselves in.

'No. It's the first place they'll look for us.'

She glanced in the mirror and we headed out of the car park. 'We need help, and we need a place of safety. You want to meet Phil Jenkinson, don't you?'

CHAPTER 5

The pine wood

We drove out to where the town becomes the country.

Angela parked in a lay-by so she could phone Phil Jenkinson. Then we phoned our parents to tell them where we were going. I could hear that Mum was really impressed.

We turned along this muddy lane to a cottage – a small, grey, stone cottage. Then, the front door swung open.

It was like falling into a paintbox.

The walls were brilliant reds and blues and spattered with posters, and in the doorway stood Phil. Really him, Phil Jenkinson, larger than life, in patched jeans and a sweatshirt.

'Angela!' he shouted. 'Nick! Tom! Come in, kettle's on. Are you hungry?'

We stood there goggle-eyed.

There were massive great plants, climbing up the walls and growing across the ceiling.

Then we heard a click and a ping and something shot into the air. I almost expected to see a flying squirrel leap from the curtains. But it was only toast jumping out of a toaster.

Phil showed us where the phone was so we could ring our parents, then he dished up tea and toast while we told him what had happened.

Then we showed him the monkeys.

He watched, fascinated, and whispered about how brilliant they were. They liked him, too. Peppy jumped on to his hand.

Then Bobtail caught hold of his beard and climbed up. Bobtail was holding something.

'Bobtail's had a baby!' said Nick.

'So they can breed in hair,' said Angela.

'Yes,' said Phil, 'but that doesn't mean it's their natural habitat.'

'Can you help?' said Nick.

'I hope so,' said Phil. 'Wildlife and television work, that's just something I do for fun. What I do for a living is to find out about rare diseases. Tropical diseases, mostly. I work for the Institute of New Virus Research. I have to find out about the sorts of diseases that might be spread by – say – rare monkeys.'

'Diseases!' Nick and I looked at each other to see if we'd got spots.

'Don't worry,' said Angela, 'I don't think the monkeys are carrying diseases.'

'But they could be,' said Phil.

'And if they did …' said Angela …

'If they carried a really puzzling, unknown disease …' said Phil, 'they'd have to be isolated … and nobody would be allowed near them …'

'Especially Professor Barron and Sir George Montgomery!' said Angela.

'Oh! Do you think they could stay here?' I asked. I couldn't help looking at the top of Phil's head.

'It's a nice idea,' he said, 'but they need to be in their own environment. They've made a home on your heads. But they must have lived somewhere else first. There must be somewhere you've been. Somewhere no one else goes.'

Angela spoke very gently. 'You told me that you'd been messing about in the park. You nearly said more to Professor Barron, but I stopped you.'

I looked at Nick. Then we both looked at our shoes.

'Whatever you tell me,' said Angela, 'nobody else needs to know. If you've done something you shouldn't, we won't be angry. But you have to tell us where you've been. We don't know how long the monkeys can live on a human head.'

I thought of Pedro. And Bobtail, and the baby. So I told Angela and Phil.

'We went to look for red squirrels on Saturday. We'd heard that there might be some in the woods at … um … Harrington Hall. It's got signs all round it saying "private" and "keep out". I suppose we were … um …'

'Trespassing?' said Angela.

'Yes. Sorry. We won't do it again.'

'I should think not,' said Phil, but he didn't seem angry. 'How would you like it if strangers just wandered into your garden? But never mind that now. Did you see any squirrels?'

'Oh, yes,' said Nick. 'There's a colony.'

'And that was Saturday,' said Angela. 'And you first found monkeys in your hair on Tuesday evening. What d'you think, Phil?'

We slept on Phil's floor that night. When we woke up, we could hear him talking on the phone.

'Hello? Professor Barron. I'm Dr Phil Jenkinson – yes, that's right, *the* Dr Jenkinson. I've been called in to see the boys with the miniature monkeys on their heads. I've put the boys straight into quarantine. And the monkeys, too. They may carry diseases. Nobody must approach them. Have you been in contact with them yourself, Professor? Oh. Don't worry, I'll arrange a course of injections for you. Contact me if you have any strange symptoms.'

He put the phone down and turned to us. 'That should keep him quiet. And Sir Monty Moneybags, too.'

'Where's Angela?'

'She's having to move fast. We need to make Harrington Hall an SSSI.'

Angela came back later, full of her news. 'It's brilliant!' she said. 'I've been to the wood and I've seen the squirrels. We were right. There are monkeys in the squirrels' coats. That's where they've come from.'

Pedro was sliding down Nick's ear. Nick was looking at something on the top of my head.

'They'll have to go back, won't they?' he said. Phil looked solemn.

'What do you think will be best for the monkeys?' he said.

'What about the winter?' I said. 'Won't they die in the cold?'

'Angela will keep watching them,' he said. 'If they're in any danger, she'll rescue them. They'd come to no harm living on her head for a while. And I'll take you to see them, now and again,' he said. 'Only remember, as far as anyone knows, we're there to watch the squirrels.'

The next morning we were all in the pine wood, with its sharp smell and its rustling sound.

We had to sit still for ages, and it was cold. We had to do that, though, so the squirrels would trust us and come close.

They're really nice looking, the red squirrels. They've got pointy ears and big brown eyes, and brushed-out tails like question marks.

There was one that kept running up to us, then changing its mind and running away again. At last it came close enough to touch.

Nick and I sat dead still. I had a furious itch in my neck. Something – probably a monkey – was tickling my ear, but I couldn't move.

The squirrel got closer. Then there was a leap, and it was on Nick's shoulder. It even poked its nose into his hair, as if it knew what to look for.

Out came Peppy and Bobtail with her baby. Then something touched my ear. I saw Kong with Tich, and Rag and Tag, all jumping on to the squirrel. They disappeared into the thick, warm coat.

Last of all, it was Pedro. I saw him for a second, swinging from one hair to another in the squirrel's tail. He looked at me. Then he climbed down a hair, and was out of sight.

He really did look right at me. I know it, I saw it. I'll be sure of it for the rest of my life.

He knew who I was, and he looked at me. And he was happy.

The squirrel dashed out of sight.

Then we stood up. It was good to get up, and get rid of the stiffness. Nick sniffed a bit, because it was so cold.

'You can come and see them again,' said Angela, 'and I'll let you know how they're doing.'

Then, as we walked back to the car, Nick said, 'Can we go home now?'

'You're supposed to be in quarantine,' said Phil, 'but you can be in quarantine at home. You can't go to school for a while, but you can have work sent to you. Yes, you can go home.'

Until Nick asked that, I hadn't realized that I wanted to go home. Now, I couldn't get there soon enough.

I was looking forward to strawberry jam on toast, sliding down the banister, watching the sports quiz with my dad.

I wanted my own room. Most of all, I was looking forward to sleeping in my own bed.

And then I knew exactly how the micro-monkeys felt when they were in my hair. I knew how they felt about going back to the squirrels.

And when I knew that, I felt better about leaving them. Even leaving Pedro.

When I got home I told Mum all about Pedro, and she really listened.

Then she said, 'Dad and I have been talking about all this. And you. And pets. I think it's time we went to the dog rescue centre.'

'Wow!' I was thrilled. I'd got used to having something that needed me.

About the author

When my children were small there were outbreaks of headlice at school, so I had to check their hair every night. Of course they hated having that 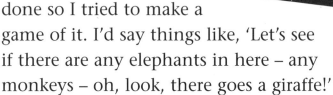 done so I tried to make a game of it. I'd say things like, 'Let's see if there are any elephants in here – any monkeys – oh, look, there goes a giraffe!'

I thought it would be fun if there really were tiny monkeys in there, swinging from one hair to another and eating bananas … and that's how this story came to be written.